THAT'S WHAT DINOSAURS DO

written by **Jory John** • illustrations by **Pete Oswald**

HARPER

An Imprint of HarperCollins Publishers

ISBN 978-0-06-234319-2

The artist used scanned watercolor textures
and digital paint to create the illustrations for this book.
Typography by Jeanne Hogle
19 20 21 22 23 SCP 10 9 8 7 6 5 4 3 2 1
❖
First Edition

To Patrick & Julie: Roar!
—J.J.

For William
—P.O.

William had a really great weekend.
But now his throat hurt from way too much roaring.

William went to the doctor.

"No more roaring for a week!" the doctor proclaimed. "And I mean it."

"ROAR?" asked William. "Exactly," said the doctor. "Don't do that."

"But how can I not roar?" thought William.

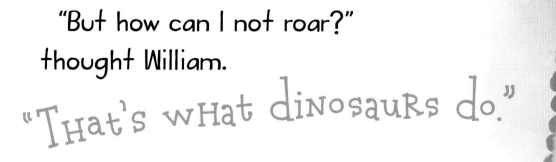

"That's what dinosaurs do."

William was sad.
Down.
Distraught.
Depressed.
Drained.
Roaring was his life!

Now wHat?

He *did* want to get better, though, so William completely stopped his roaring.

It was not easy.

There were just so many great opportunities to roar.

SIGHHHHH.

As embarrassing as it was, poor William decided that he must live a life of silence. He sat in his chair and stared at the wall and drank cup after cup of chamomile tea with honey.

"Not roaring is so *boring*," thought William.

It's no fun when a dinosaur loses his roar. Even for a week!

On Tuesday,

On Wednesday,

William moped around
his garden.

William remained inside
his house.

On Thursday,

On Friday,

William stayed under
the covers . . . all day.

William could barely stand it.
He *had* to roar again.

William went back to
the doctor.

"It looks a little better, William," said the doctor. "Still not great, though."

"ROAR?"

asked William.

"You may roar," said the doctor. "But if you roar too much, your throat will surely hurt again."

Outside the doctor's office, William spotted the mailman, who smiled and waved. William waved back.

Then he felt something bubbling up inside of him.

William knew he shouldn't roar at the nice mailman.

But he did it anyway.

"ROAARRRRRR!"

Because that's what dinosaurs do.

William spotted some kids at the playground.

They were having a lot of fun. William liked fun. So
he joined them on the swings. And on the slide.

While he played, William
knew he shouldn't roar at all
the kids.
 But then he felt a new roar
bubbling up . . .

until . . .

he just couldn't help himself.

"ROAARRRRRR!"

Because that's what dinosaurs do.

William spotted some people waiting for the bus. He waited.

FACT: DINOSAURS DON'T LIKE WAITING.

And waited.

FACT: THEY LIKE ROARING.

"ROAAR

RRRRR!"

Yes, that's what dinosaurs do!

William rode the bus all the way home.
At his stop, the driver said, "Have a nice weekend, William."

William turned and smiled his nicest, toothiest smile.

Then he roared in the driver's face.

"ROAARRRRRR!"

18TH STREET

"Geez!
What was
that for?"
asked the driver.

There was only one answer to his question:

"That's what dinosaurs do."

The townspeople gathered in front of
William's house and demanded an apology.
Even his doctor was there.

But William wasn't sorry for roaring.
Not one bit.
You want to know why?

BECAUSE THAT'S WHAT DINOSAURS DO.